Aesop's Fables

The Ant and the Grasshopper

By George Carvalho

Published by
George Carvalho
Animaza Studios
Miami, Florida
www.animaza.com

1

There once was a grasshopper
who liked to play with his flute.

2

ts,

"What are you doing?" asked the grasshopper,
wanting to know.

4

"We are gathering food for the winter,"
they replied, "before it starts to snow."

5

6

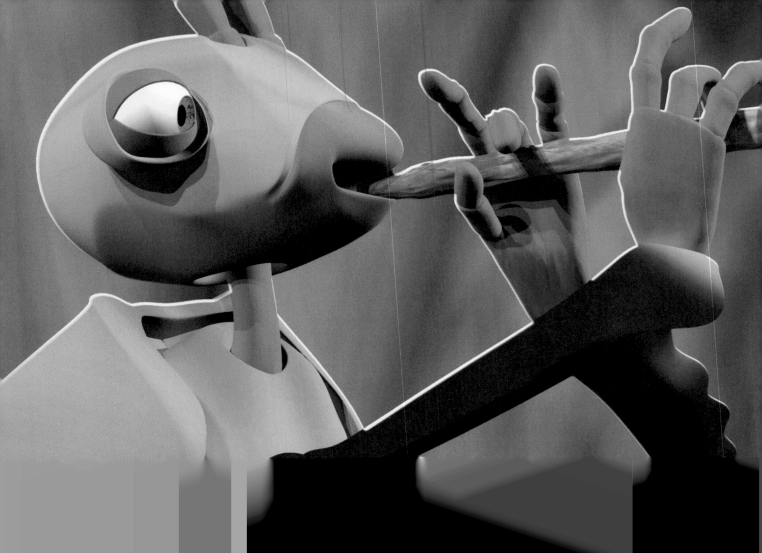

while the ants had to carry apples
and peaches and even a pear.

That made the ant angry
but then it started to snow.

The ant took the berry back,
and quickly ran away

while the grasshopper took his flute
and continued to play.

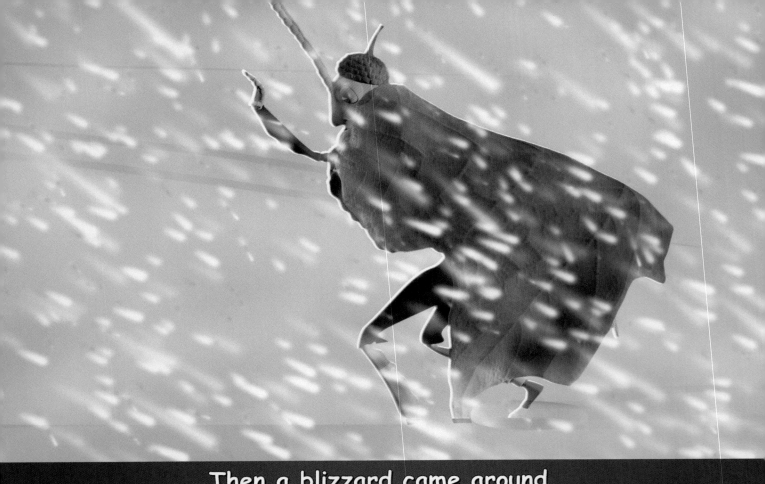

Then a blizzard came around,
and the grasshopper had nothing to eat.

So he went to see the ants home,
hoping to meet.

14

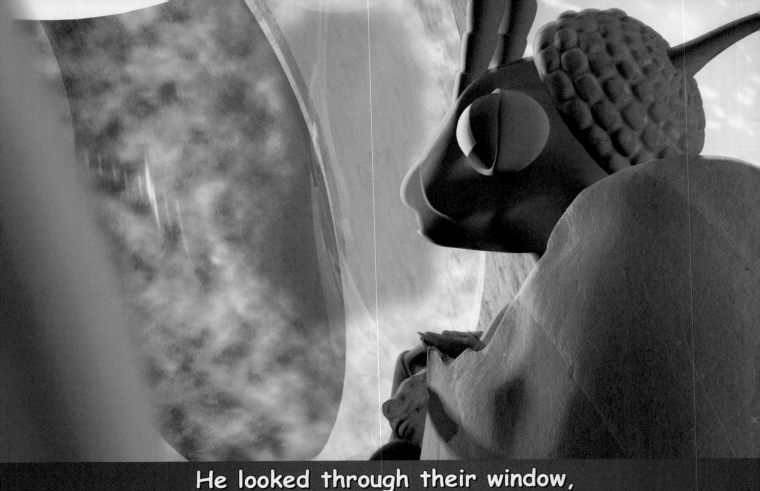

He looked through their window,
and what did he see?

He saw ants laughing and eating
and all full of glee.

17

18

the ant he met earlier, now wondering
what the grasshopper was here for.

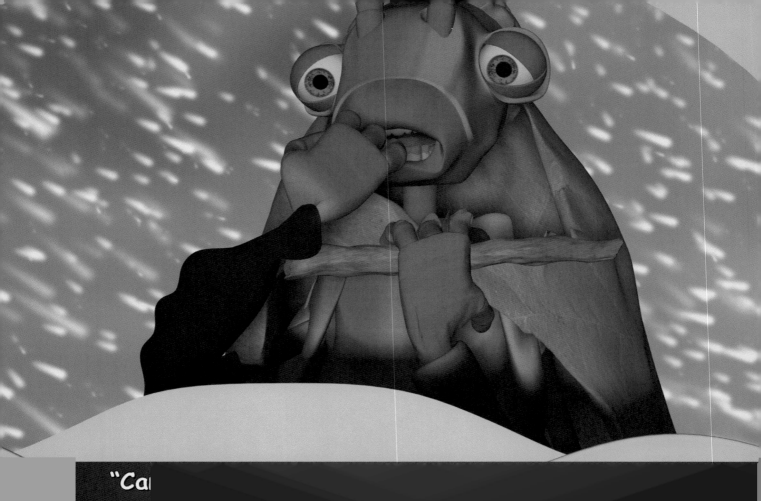

"Ca

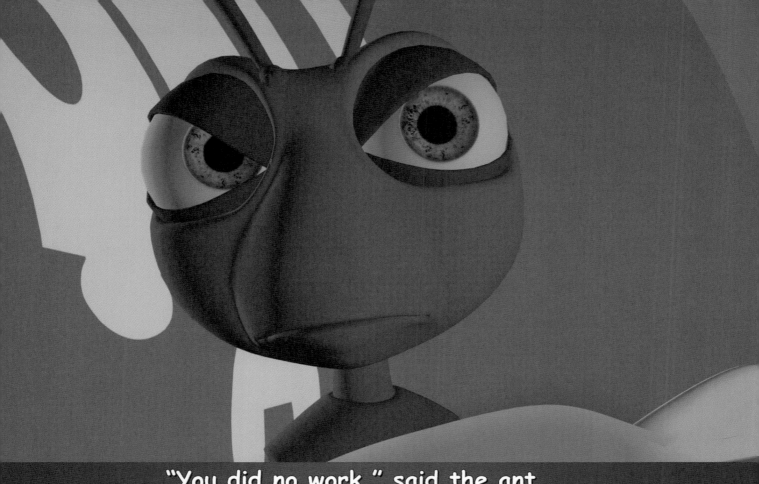

"You did no work," said the ant,
"so no food for you, and it serves you right!"   22

But he learned his lesson next summer,
and was now in the know.

24

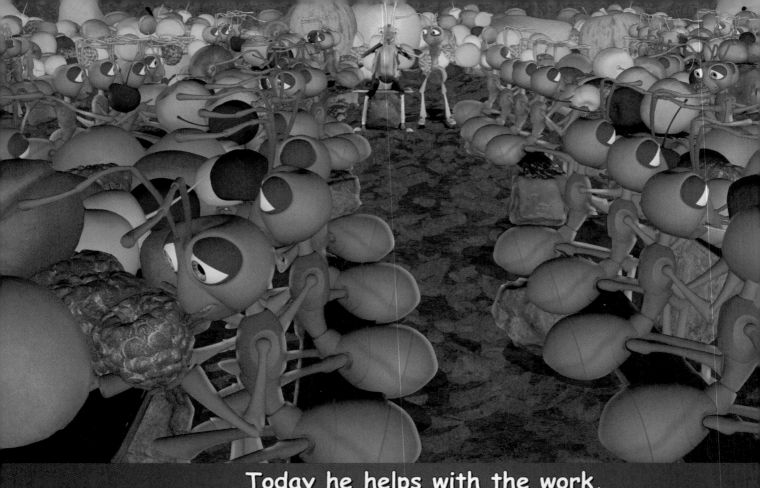

Today he helps with the work,
and has made amends.

25

And now spends winters with the ants,
his newfound friends.

26

Watch the movie!

Aesop's Fables
The Ant and the Grasshopper
Short Film

Head over to
Animaza.com
to watch the
Short Film
based on the story.

ANIMAZA
S T U D I O S
animaza.com

Printed in Great Britain
by Amazon